First published in Great Britain in 2020 by Gollancz
an imprint of The Orion Publishing Group Ltd
Carmelite House, 50 Victoria Embankment, London EC4Y 0DZ

An Hachette UK Company

1 3 5 7 9 10 8 6 4 2

A CIP catalogue record for this book is

available from the British Library.

ISBN (Hardback) 978 1 473 22430 2

Typeset by Amanda Cummings
Printed in Italy

www.gollancz.co.uk

The
Ankh-Morpork City Watch
DISCWORLD JOURNAL

USEFUL INFORMATION FOR WATCHMEN IN THE FIELD, ON THE BEAT OR IN A BIND.

Being, at best, a quick reference guide. You are reminded that it is the duty of every Watchman to familiarise themselves with emergency procedures and to be prepared mentally and physically for the most treacherous of situations. Should you require further instruction as to the definition of such situations, please report to 'The Old Lemonade Factory' at Pseudopolis Yard, where you shall be aquainted with some.

MAJOR WATCH HOUSES:

Being those which are open to Watchmen at all hours, connected by clacks to all subsidiary premises and where Watchmen can find an officer ranked at or above Sergeant at all times. As an officer of the City Watch you may report to all/any of these Watch Houses for assistance. Once you have presented your badge to the officer on duty, such assistance and courtesy as would be reasonably afforded without regard to species, religious persuasion or external evidence of corporeal activity (vital status) should be expected e.g. advice or aid (of a professional or medical nature) or for shelter from extreme weather, angry mobs, marauding barbarian hordes or Mrs. Cake.

TREACLE MINE ROAD
CABLE STREET
CHITTLING STREET
DIMWELL STREET
DOLLY SISTERS
KINGS WAY
LEASTGATE
LONG WALL
NAP HILL
BROAD WAY

It is advisable, but not manditory, that you make a donation to the Tea Kitty when visiting another Watch House.

I OWN YOU
3P
NOBBY

STANDARD OFFICER'S EQUIPTMENT:

You are reminded that it is your individual responsibility to maintain and account for your standard issue equiptment.

One (1) Shirt, Mail, Chain
One (1) Helmet, Iron and Copper
One (1) Breastplate, Iron and Copper
Breeches, Knee, Leather, Watch Officers for the use of
Cape, Rain, Leather, Watch Officers for the use of
Sandals, Leather, Watch Officers for the use of (Summer)
Boots, Leather, Watch Officers for the use of (Winter)
One (1) Sword, Short, or:
(One (1) Axe, Standard Battle, Dwarf Officers for the use of
One (1) Club, Troll Officers for the use of)
One (1) Stave, Oak
One (1) Pike or Halberd
One (1) Crossbow
Three (3) bolts, Crossbow
One (1) Hourglass
One (1) Bell, Hand, Brass and Oak
One (1) Pot Ceramic Cement, Golem Officers, for the use of
One (1) Badge, Office of, Watchmans, Copper

Inspections may be called at any time, (without prior warning) at which point you will be expected to present said equiptment, without a delay of more than one hour, in a condition satisfying the commanding officer's expectations (I.O.U.'s and pawnbroker's receipts are no longer acceptable).

Any loss of, or damage to, City Watch property is to be reported immediately, and will require a completed A-M:cw/0992 form, endorsed by a senior officer (excl. Cpl. Nobbs). This is to be submitted, along with a signed statement from the officer or his next of kin, to A.E Pessimal, Inspector of the Watch, Pseudopolis Yard.

You retain the right to purchase your own equiptment, so long as it meets Watch requirements. If it is considerably superior to that of other serving officers you may be required not to flash it around. This is for your own protection.

I,

[recruit's name...............................],
do solemnly swear by [recruit's deity of
choice..]
to uphold the Laws and Ordinances of
the City of Ankh-Morpork, serve the
public truſt, and defend the ſubjects
of His/Her (delete whichever is
inappropriate) Majesty (name of
reigning monarch................................)
without fear, favour, or thought of
personal ſafety; to purſue evildoers
and protect the innocent, laying down
my life if neceſsary in the cauſe of
said duty, so help me (aforeſaid deity).
Gods Save the King/Queen (delete
whichever is inappropriate).

Vimes sighed inwardly. He had a notebook. He took notes in it. It was always useful. And then Sybil, gods bless her, had bought him this fifteen-function imp which did so many other things, although as far as he could see at least ten of its functions consisted of apologising for its inefficiency.

~ Terry Pratchett, *Feet of Clay*

STATEMENT

Lord Vetinari on Vimes

'We need to know the *truth*, Vimes. Commander Sam Vimes's truth. It may count for more than you think. In the Plains, certainly, and much further. People know about you, commander. Descendant of a Watchman who believed that if a corrupted court will not behead an evil king, then the Watchman should do it himself—'

'It was only *one* king,' Vimes protested.

~ Terry Pratchett, *Thud!*

STATEMENT

. . . Commander Vimes didn't like the phrase 'The innocent have nothing to fear', believing the innocent had everything to fear, mostly from the guilty but in the longer term even more from those who say things like 'The innocent have nothing to fear' . . .

~ Terry Pratchett, *Snuff*

STATEMENT

Vimes stalked gloomily through the crowded streets, feeling like the only pickled onion in a fruit salad.

~ Terry Pratchett, *Guards! Guards!*

STATEMENT

Vimes snorted. I grew up here, he thought, and when I walk down the street everyone says, 'Who's that glum bugger?' Carrot's been here a few months and everyone knows him. And he knows everyone. Everyone likes him. I'd be annoyed about that, if only he wasn't so likeable.

~ Terry Pratchett, *Men at Arms*

STATEMENT

Angua discusses gender politics with Cheery Littlebottom

'It's like that in the Watch, too,' said Angua. 'You can be any sex you
like provided you act male. There's no men and women in the Watch,
just a bunch of lads. You'll soon learn the language. Basically it's how
much beer you supped last night, how strong the curry was you had
afterwards, and where you were sick. Just think egotesticle.'

~ Terry Pratchett, *Feet of Clay*

The reason that the rich were so rich, Vimes reasoned, was because they managed to spend less money.

Take boots, for example. He earned thirty-eight dollars a month plus allowances. A really good pair of leather boots cost fifty dollars. But an *affordable* pair of boots, which were sort of OK for a season or two and then leaked like hell when the cardboard gave out, cost about ten dollars. Those were the kind of boots Vimes always bought, and wore until the soles were so thin that he could tell where he was in Ankh-Morpork on a foggy night by the feel of the cobbles.

But the thing was that *good* boots lasted for years and years. A man who could afford fifty dollars had a pair of boots that'd still be keeping his feet dry in ten years' time, while a poor man who could only afford cheap boots would have spent a hundred dollars on boots in the same time and *would still have wet feet.*

This was the Captain Samuel Vimes 'Boots' theory of socio-economic unfairness.

~ Terry Pratchett, *Men at Arms*

STATEMENT

It always amazed Vimes how Nobby got along with practically everyone. It must, he'd decided, have something to do with the common denominator. In the entire world of mathematics there could be no denominator as common as Nobby.

~ Terry Pratchett, *Guards! Guards!*

STATEMENT

Sergeant Colon had had a broad education. He'd been to the School of My Dad Always Said, the College of It Stands to Reason, and was now a postgraduate student at the University of What Some Bloke In the Pub Told Me.

~ Terry Pratchett, *Jingo*

STATEMENT

His job was to make sense of the world,
and there were times when he wished
that the world would meet him halfway.

~ Terry Pratchett, *Snuff*

STATEMENT

Vimes felt a sudden surge of civic pride. There had to be something right about a citizenry which, when faced with catastrophe, thought about selling sausages to the participants.

~ Terry Pratchett, *Guards! Guards!*

STATEMENT

Who knew what evil lurked in the hearts of men? A copper, that's who.

~ Terry Pratchett, *Night Watch*

Samuel Vimes dreamed about Clues. He had a jaundiced view of Clues. He instinctively distrusted them. They got in the way.

And he distrusted the kind of person who'd take one look at another man and say in a lordly voice to his companion, 'Ah, my dear sir, I can tell you nothing except that he is a left-handed stonemason who has spent some years in the merchant navy and has recently fallen on hard times,' and then unroll a lot of supercilious commentary about calluses and stance and the state of a man's boots, when *exactly the same* comments could apply to a man who was wearing his old clothes because he'd been doing a spot of home bricklaying for a new barbecue pit, and had been tattooed once when he was drunk and seventeen* and in fact got seasick on a wet pavement. What arrogance! What an insult to the rich and chaotic variety of the human experience!

*These terms are often synonymous.

~ Terry Pratchett, *Feet of Clay*

STATEMENT

... 'It is to be hoped that things will improve, however, and Uberwald will, happily, be joining the community of nations.'

Vimes and Vetinari exchanged looks. Sometimes Carrot sounded like a civics essay written by a stunned choirboy.

~ Terry Pratchett, *The Fifth Elephant*

STATEMENT

. . . 'here's some advice, boy. Don't put your trust in revolutions. They always come around again. That's why they're called revolutions. People die, and nothing changes.'

~ Terry Pratchett, *Night Watch*

Coppers were always outnumbered, so being a copper only worked when people let it work. If they refocused and realised you were just another standard idiot with a pennyworth of metal for a badge, you could end up a smear on the pavement.

~ Terry Pratchett, *Night Watch*

STATEMENT

'Might have just been an innocent bystander, sir,' said Carrot.
   'What, in Ankh-Morpork?'
   'Yes, sir.'
   'We should have grabbed him, then, just for the rarity value.'

~ Terry Pratchett, *Guards! Guards!*

STATEMENT

Vimes sighed. He was an honest man. He'd always felt that was one of the bigger defects in his personality.

~ Terry Pratchett, *Feet of Clay*

STATEMENT

Sergeant Colon owed thirty years of happy marriage to the fact that
Mrs Colon worked all day and Sergeant Colon worked all night.
They communicated by means of notes. He got her tea ready before
he left at night, she left his breakfast nice and hot in the oven in the
mornings. They had three grown-up children, all born, Vimes had
assumed, as a result of extremely persuasive handwriting.

~ Terry Pratchett, *Guards! Guards!*

STATEMENT

'You'll be upholding the honour of
Ankh-Morpork, remember!'
　'Really, dear? What shall I do
with the other hand?' said Vimes.

~ Terry Pratchett, *Thud!*

....

....

....

....

....

....

....

....

....

'I fink, derefore
I am. I fink.'

~ Terry Pratchett,
Where's My Cow?

Keep the peace. That was the thing. People often failed to understand what that meant. You'd go to some life-threatening disturbance like a couple of neighbours scrapping in the street over who owned the hedge between their properties, and they'd both be bursting with aggrieved self-righteousness, both yelling, their wives would either be having a private scrap on the side or would have adjourned to a kitchen for a shared pot of tea and a chat, and they all expected you to *sort it out*.

And they could never understand that it wasn't your job. Sorting it out was a job for a good surveyor and a couple of lawyers, maybe. *Your* job was to quell the impulse to bang their stupid fat heads together, to ignore the affronted speeches of dodgy self-justification, to get them to stop shouting and to get them off the street. Once that had been achieved, your job was over. You weren't some walking god, dispensing finely tuned natural justice. Your job was simply to bring back peace.

~ Terry Pratchett, *Night Watch*

STATEMENT

'It's a far, far better thing I do now than I have ever done before,' said Nobby.

'Right,' said Sergeant Colon. They walked on in silence for a while and he added: 'O' course, that's not difficult.'

~ Terry Pratchett, *Jingo*

STATEMENT

Sergeant Colon of the Ankh-Morpork City Guard was on duty. He was guarding the Brass Bridge, the main link between Ankh and Morpork. From theft.

When it came to crime prevention, Sergeant Colon found it safest to think big.

~ Terry Pratchett, *Reaper Man*

STATEMENT

On the traditional Watchman's walk

The legs swung, the feet moved, the mind began to work in a certain way. It wasn't a dream state, exactly. It was just that the ears, nose and eyeballs wired themselves straight into the ancient 'suspicious bastard' node of his brain, leaving his higher brain-centre free to freewheel.

~ Terry Pratchett, *Jingo*

STATEMENT

'Didn't know what'd hit 'em, eh?' said Vimes.

Detritus looked mildly offended at this. 'Oh no, sir,' he said, 'I made sure they knew I hit 'em.'

~ Terry Pratchett, *Thud!*

STATEMENT

Vimes had once discussed the Ephebian idea
of 'democracy' with Carrot and had been rather
interested in the idea that everyone had a vote until
he found out that while he, Vimes, would have a
vote, there was no way in the rules that anyone
could prevent Nobby Nobbs from having one as well.

~ Terry Pratchett, *The Fifth Elephant*

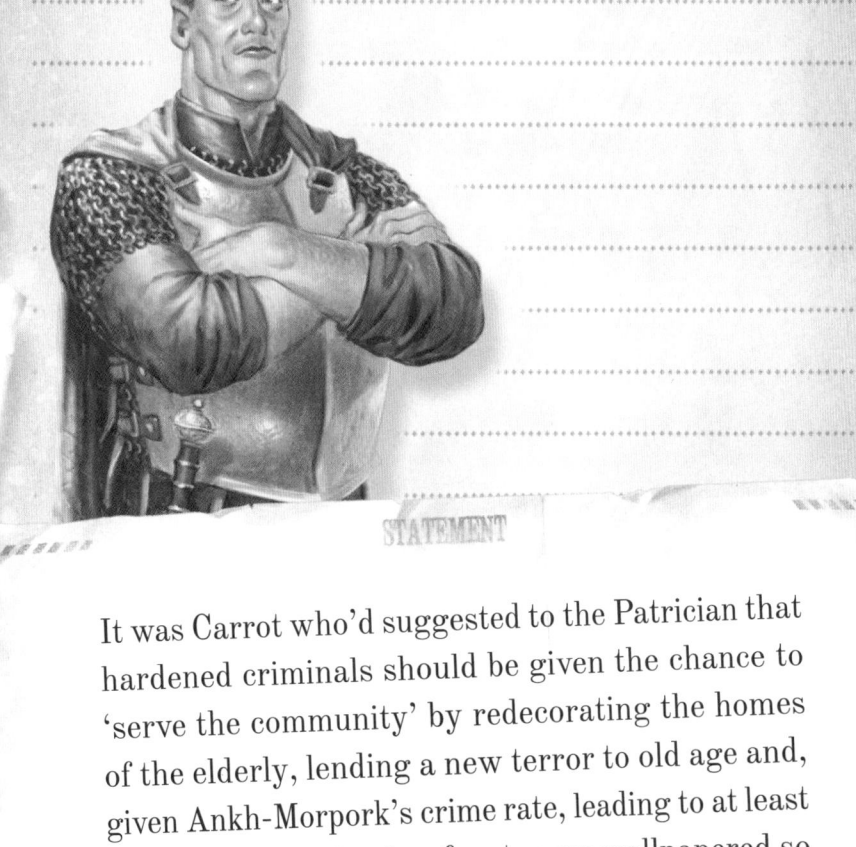

STATEMENT

It was Carrot who'd suggested to the Patrician that hardened criminals should be given the chance to 'serve the community' by redecorating the homes of the elderly, lending a new terror to old age and, given Ankh-Morpork's crime rate, leading to at least one old lady having her front room wallpapered so many times in six months that now she could only get in sideways.

~ Terry Pratchett, *Feet of Clay*

STATEMENT

A match flared in the dark, and they turned to see Vimes light a cigar.

'You'd like Freedom, Truth and Justice, wouldn't you, comrade sergeant?' said Reg encouragingly.

'I'd like a hard-boiled egg,' said Vimes, shaking the match out.

~ Terry Pratchett, *Night Watch*

On the importance of six o'clock

He shut his eyes and then, hearing a change in the sound of the wheels, risked opening them again.

The coach flew across the junction. Vimes had a momentary glimpse of a huge queue, fuming and shouting behind a couple of immovable troll officers, before they were spinning on down towards Scoone Avenue.

'You closed the road? You closed the road!' he yelled, above the wind.

'And Kings Way, sir. Just in case,' Carrot shouted down.

'You closed *two* major roads? Two whole damn roads? In the rush hour?'

'Yes, sir,' said Carrot. 'It was the only way.'

Vimes hung on, speechless. Would *he* have dared do that? But that was Carrot all over. There was a problem, and now it's gone. Admittedly, the whole city is probably solid with wagons by now, but that's a *new* problem.

He'd be home in time. Would a minute have mattered? No, probably not, although Young Sam appeared to have a very accurate internal clock. Possibly even two minutes would be okay. Three minutes, even. You could go to five, perhaps. But that was just it. If you could go to five minutes then you'd go to ten, then half an hour, a couple of hours . . . and not see your son all evening. So that was that. Six o'clock, prompt. Every day. Read to Young Sam. No excuses. He'd promised himself that. *No excuses.* No excuses at all. Once you had a good excuse, you opened the door to bad excuses.

~ Terry Pratchett, *Thud*

STATEMENT

He kept the cell keys in a tin box in the bottom drawer of his desk, a long way out of reach of any stick, hand, dog, cunningly thrown belt or trained Klatchian monkey spider*.

*Making Fred Colon possibly unique in the annals of jail history.

~ Terry Pratchett, *Thud!*

STATEMENT

Vimes defends Dorfl, Ankh-Morpork's first golem Watchman

The Patrician waved a hand towards the stairs and his office full of paper. 'Nevertheless, Commander, I've had no less than nine missives from leading religious figures declaring that he is an abomination.'

'Yes, sir. I've given that viewpoint a lot of thought, sir, and reached the following conclusion: arseholes to the lot of 'em, sir.'

~ Terry Pratchett, *Feet of Clay*

STATEMENT

It was Angua's mind that prowled the night, not a werewolf mind. She was almost entirely sure of that. A werewolf wouldn't stop at chickens, not by a long way.

She shuddered.

Who was she kidding? It was easy to be a vegetarian by day, It was preventing yourself becoming a humanitarian at night that took the real effort.

~ Terry Pratchett, *Feet of Clay*

....

....

....

....

....

....

....

....

....

....

....

STATEMENT

People would probably say they had lived blameless lives.
But Vimes was a policeman. *No one* lived a completely
blameless life. It might be just possible, by lying very still in a
cellar somewhere, to get through a day without committing a crime.
But only just. And, even then, you were probably guilty of loitering.

~ Terry Pratchett, *Feet of Clay*

....

....

....

....

....

....

....

....

....

....

STATEMENT

Detritus's intelligence
wasn't too bad for a
troll, falling somewhere
between a cuttlefish and
a line-dancer, but you
could rely on him not to
let it slow him down.

~ Terry Pratchett, *Jingo*

STATEMENT

It was so much easier to blame it on Them. It was bleakly depressing to think that They were Us. If it was Them, then nothing was anyone's fault. If it was Us, what did that make Me? After all, I'm one of Us. I must be. I've certainly never thought of myself as one of Them. *No one* ever thinks of themselves as one of Them. We're always one of Us. It's Them that do the bad things.

~ Terry Pratchett, *Jingo*

STATEMENT

'They always give *me* bath salts,' complained Nobby.
'And bath soap and bubble bath and herbal bath lumps
and tons of bath stuff and I can't think why, 'cos it's not
as if I hardly ever *has* a bath. You'd think they'd take
the hint, wouldn't you?'

~ Terry Pratchett, *Hogfather*

It wasn't proper police work, Vimes considered, unless you were doing something that someone somewhere would much rather you weren't doing.

~ Terry Pratchett, *Jingo*

Two uniformed trolls were standing in front of Sergeant Colon's high desk, with a slightly smaller troll between them. This troll was wearing a slightly downcast expression. It was also wearing a tutu and had a small pair of gauzed wings glued to its back.

'—happen to know that trolls don't have *any* tradition of a Tooth Fairy,' Colon was saying. 'Especially not one called' – he looked down – "Clinkerbell". So how about we just call it breaking and entering without a Thieves' Guild license?'

'Is racial prejudice, not letting trolls have a Tooth Fairy,' Clinkerbell muttered.

One of the troll guards upended a sack on the desk. Various items of silverwear cascaded over the paperwork.

'And this is what you found under their pillows, was it?' said Colon.

'Bless dere little hearts,' said Clinkerbell.

~ Terry Pratchett, *Feet of Clay*

AMCW

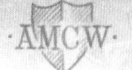

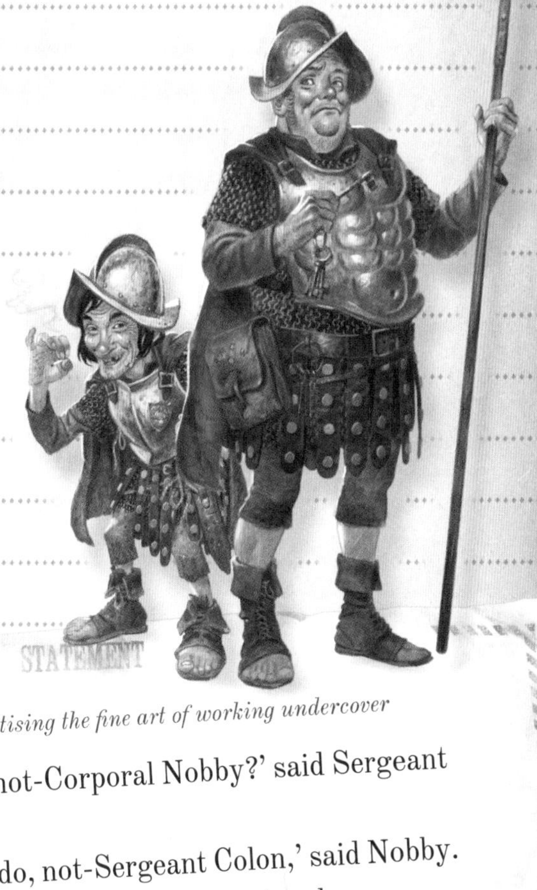

STATEMENT

Nobby and Colon practising the fine art of working undercover

'Have another drink, not-Corporal Nobby?' said Sergeant Colon unsteadily.

'I do not mind if I do, not-Sergeant Colon,' said Nobby. They were taking inconspicuosity seriously.

~ Terry Pratchett, *Guards! Guards!*

STATEMENT

Odd thing, ain't it . . . you meet people one
at a time, they seem decent, they got brains
that work, and then they get together and you
hear the *voice* of the people. And it snarls.

~ Terry Pratchett, *Jingo*

STATEMENT

I'll have to go, Angua thought as they strolled on down the street. *Sooner or later he'll see that it can't really work out. Werewolves and humans . . . we've both got too much to lose. Sooner or later I'll have to leave him.* But, for one day at a time, let it be tomorrow.

~ Terry Pratchett, *Feet of Clay*

STATEMENT

But the helmet had gold decoration, and the bespoke armourers had made a new gleaming breastplate with useless gold ornamentation on it. Sam Vimes felt like a class traitor every time he wore it. He hated being thought of as one of those people that wore stupid ornamental armour. It was gilt by association.

~ Terry Pratchett, *Night Watch*

'Well, Nobby, you're what I might call a career soldier, right?'

'S'right, Fred.'

'How many dishonourable discharges have you had?'

'Lots,' said Nobby, proudly. 'But I always puts a poultice on 'em.'

~ Terry Pratchett, *Men at Arms*

....

....

....

....

....

....

....

....

....

....

STATEMENT

'Were you proposing to shoot these people in cold blood, sergeant?'

'Nossir. Just a warning shot inna head, sir.'

~ Terry Pratchett, *Jingo*

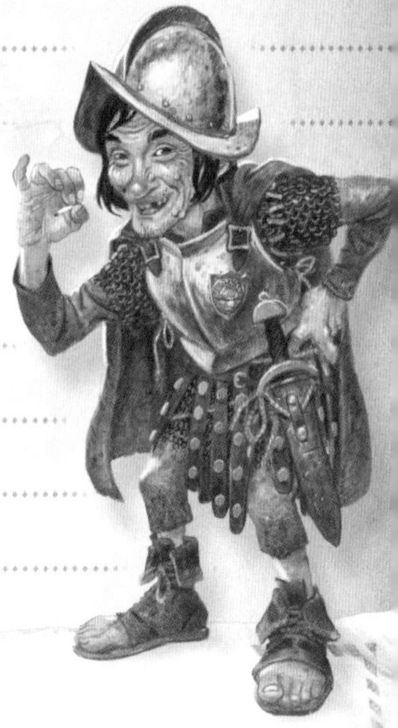

STATEMENT

Nobby was human, just like many other officers. It was just that he was the only one who had to carry a certificate to prove it.

~ Terry Pratchett, *Night Watch*

I, after hearing evidence from a number of experts, including Mrs Slugary the midwife, certify that the balance of probability is that the bearer of this document, C.M.O.T. StJohn Nobbs, is a human being.

Signed, Lord X ....

Willikins and Sybil between them conspired to prevent him wearing old, well-worn boots these da— those days, and stole them away in the night to have the soles repaired. It was good to *feel* the streets with dry feet again. And after a lifetime of walking them, he did *feel* the streets. There were the cobblestones: catheads, trollheads, loaves, short and long setts, rounders, Morpork Sixes, and the eighty-seven types of paving brick, and the fourteen types of stone slab, and the twelve types of stone never intended for street slabs which had got used anyway, and had their own patterns of wear, and the rubbles and the gravels, and the repairs, and the thirteen different types of cellar cover and twenty types of drain lid—

He bounced a little, like a man testing the hardness of something. 'Elm Street,' he said. He bounced again. 'Junction with Twinkle. Yeah.'

He was back.

~ Terry Pratchett, *Night Watch*

....

....

....

....

....

....

....

....

....

....

....

Carrot often struck people as simple. And he was. Where people went wrong was thinking that simple meant the same thing as stupid.

~ Terry Pratchett, *Men at Arms*

STATEMENT

. . . Sergeant Colon did know the meaning of the word 'irony'. He thought it meant 'sort of like iron'.

~ Terry Pratchett, *Reaper Man*

STATEMENT

'Carrot, I think you've got something wrong with your head,' said Angua.

'What?'

'I think you may have got it stuck up your bum . . .'

~ Terry Pratchett, *Feet of Clay*

STATEMENT

'Commander, I always used to consider that you had a definite anti-authoritarian streak in you.'

'Sir?'

'It seems that you have managed to retain this even though you *are* authority.'

'Sir?'

'That's practically zen.'

~ Terry Pratchett, *Feet of Clay*

STATEMENT

'Sixty new officers?' said Lord Vetinari.

'The price of peace, sir,' said Captain Carrot earnestly. 'I'm sure that Commander Vimes wouldn't settle for anything less. We are really stretched.'

'Sixty men – and dwarfs and trolls, obviously – is more than a third of your current complement,' said the Patrician, tapping his walking stick on the cobbles. 'Peace comes with a rather large bill, captain.'

'And a few dividends, sir,' Carrot said.

~ Terry Pratchett, *Thud!*

STATEMENT

Colon had always thought that heroes had some
special kind of clockwork that made them go out
and die famously for god, country, and apple pie,
or whatever particular delicacy their mother made.
It had never occurred to him that they might do it
because they'd get yelled at if they didn't.

~ Terry Pratchett, *Jingo*

STATEMENT

'What did I tell you about
Mister Safety Catch?' said
Vimes weakly.
    'When Mister Safety Catch
Is Not On, Mister Crossbow
Is Not Your Friend,' recited
Detritus, saluting.

~ Terry Pratchett, *Night Watch*

These were dangerous thoughts, he knew. They were the kind that crept up on a Watchman when the chase was over and it was just you and him, facing one another in that breathless little pinch between the crime and the punishment.

And maybe a Watchman had seen civilisation with the skin ripped off one time too many and stopped acting like a Watchman and started acting like a normal human being and realised that the click of the crossbow or the sweep of the sword would make all the world so *clean*.

And you couldn't think like that, even about vampires. Even though they'd take the lives of other people because little lives don't matter and what the hell can we take away from *them*?

And you couldn't think like that because they gave you a sword and a badge and that turned you into something else and *that* had to mean there were some thoughts you couldn't think.

Only crimes could take place in darkness. Punishment had to be done in the light. That was the job of a good Watchman, Carrot always said. To light a candle in the dark.

~ Terry Pratchett, *Feet of Clay*

STATEMENT

Sometimes it's better to light a flamethrower than curse the darkness.

~ Terry Pratchett, *Men at Arms*

AMCW

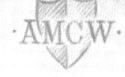

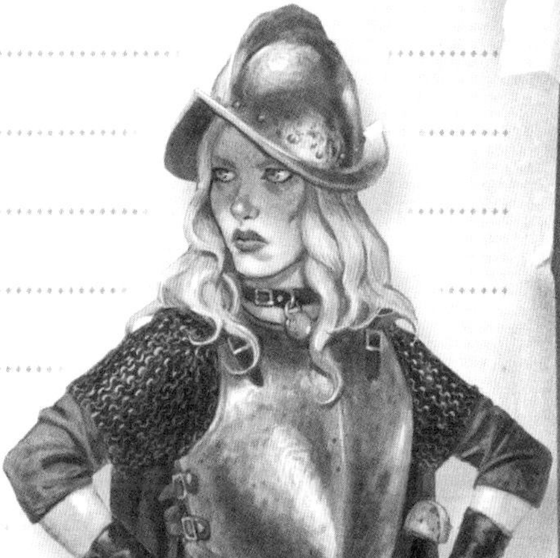

STATEMENT

'Look, sir, I know Angua. She's not the useless type. She doesn't stand there and scream helplessly. She makes other people do that.'

~ Terry Pratchett, *Jingo*

STATEMENT

It wasn't that he'd *liked* being shot at by hooded figures in the temporary employ of his many and varied enemies, but he'd always looked at it as some kind of vote of confidence. It showed that he was annoying the rich and arrogant people who ought to be annoyed.

~ Terry Pratchett, *Night Watch*

STATEMENT

... 'Let this be a lesson, lad. There aren't any rules. Not when there's knives out. You take him down, quietly if possible, without hurting him much if possible, but you take him down. He comes at you with a knife, you bring your stick down on his arm. He comes at you with his hands, you use your knee or your boot or your helmet. Your job is to keep the peace. You make it peaceful as quickly as you can.'

~ Terry Pratchett, *Night Watch*

STATEMENT

People expected all kinds of things from coppers,
but there was one thing that sooner or later they
all wanted: make this not be happening.
Make this not be happening . . .

~ Terry Pratchett, *Night Watch*

And Sam Vimes ran. He tore off his cloak and whirled away his plumed hat, and he ran and ran.

There would be trouble later on. People would ask questions. But that was later on – for now, gloriously uncomplicated and wonderfully clean, and hopefully with never an end, under a clear sky, in a world untarnished . . . there was only the chase.

~ Terry Pratchett, *Jingo*

ALL THE LITTLE ANGELS rise up, rise up,
All the little angels rise up high!
How do they rise up, rise up,
How do they rise up high?
They rise heads up, heads up,
they rise heads up, heads up high!

All the little angels rise up, rise up,
All the little angels rise up high!
How do they rise up, rise up,
How do they rise up high?
They rise knees up, knees up,
they rise knees up, knees up high!

All the little angels rise up, rise up,
All the little angels rise up high!
How do they rise up, rise up,
How do they rise up high?
They rise feet up, feet up,
they rise feet up, feet up high!

All the little angels rise up, rise up,
All the little angels rise up high!
How do they rise up, rise up,
How do they rise up high?
They rise arse up, arse up,
they rise arse up, arse up high!

~ Terry Pratchett, *Night Watch*